Allah Gave Me
TWO EARS TO HEAR

Amrana Arif

Illustrated by Asiya Clarke

THE ISLAMIC FOUNDATION

Allah Gave Me Two Ears to Hear

The alarm clock that goes beep, beep, beep!
It wakes me up from my deep deep sleep.

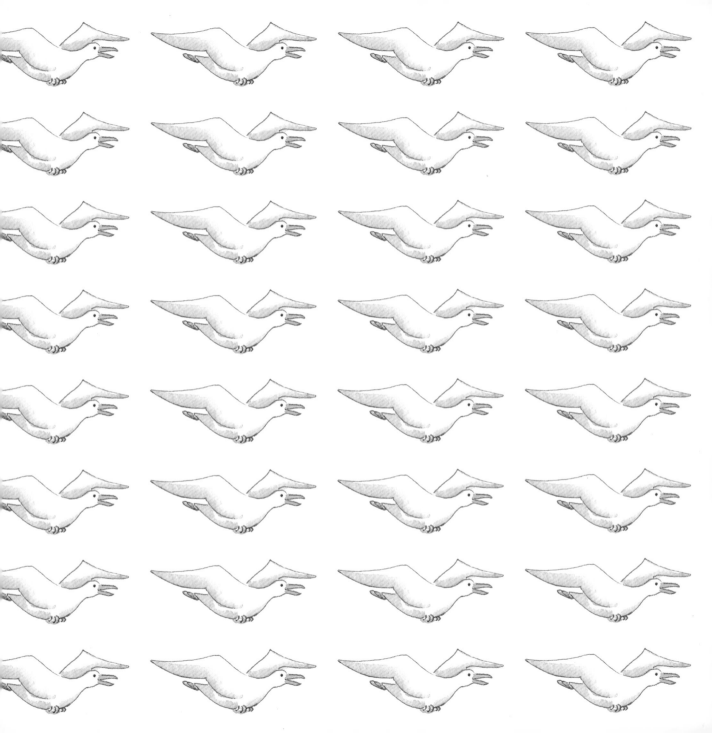

Copyright of The Islamic Foundation. 2003 / 1424 AH.
Third impression 2015 / 1436 H

ISBN: 978-0-86037-353-7

MUSLIM CHILDREN'S LIBRARY

ALLAH THE MAKER SERIES

Allah Gave Me Two Ears To Hear

Author: *Amrana Arif*
Illustrator: *Asiya Clarke*
Designer: *Steven Stratford*
Co-ordinator: *Raana Bokhari*

Published by
THE ISLAMIC FOUNDATION
Markfield Conference Centre, Ratby Lane, Markfield
Leicestershire, LE67 9SY, United Kingdom
E-mail: publications@islamic-foundation.com
Website: www.islamic-foundation.com

Quran House, P.O. Box 30611, Nairobi, Kenya

P.M.B. 3193, Kano, Nigeria

Distributed by
Kube Publishing Ltd.
Tel: +44(01530) 249230, Fax: +44(01530) 249656
E-mail: info@kubepublishing.com
Website: www.kubepublishing.com

Printed by Imak Offset, Turkey

British Library Cataloguing in Publication Data

Arif, Amrana
Allah Gave me two ears to hear. - (Allah the maker series)
1. Hearing - Juvenile literature 2. Hearing - Religious aspects -
Islam - Juvenile literature 3. Ear - Juvenile literature
4. Ear - Religious aspects - Islam - Juvenile literature
I. Title II. Islamic Foundation
612.8'5
ISBN 978-0-86037-353-7

Daddy recites the Qur'an in the morning,
He says the Book gives good news and a warning.

Allah Gave Me Two Ears to Hear

The pretty birds chirping their musical song;
They sing and praise Allah all day long.

The rustling of the fallen autumn leaves,
Awakened by the cool fresh breeze.

Allah Gave Me Two Ears to Hear

The rumbling of my hungry tummy
Makes me quickly look for my Mummy!

The rattling of the colourful pots,
My Mummy makes breakfast and I eat lots!

Allah Gave Me Two Ears to Hear

The pitter-patter of my brother's feet,
As he runs to the table ready to eat.

The whistle of the kettle when the water is hot.
My Daddy makes tea in the big tea-pot!

Allah Gave Me Two Ears to Hear

The splish-splash of waves of blue sea water!
I swim to cool down as the day gets hotter.

So many creatures on the beach to be found,
Each praising Allah with their own special sound.

Allah Gave Me Two Ears to Hear

The buzzing in summer of the black and yellow bees,
As they fly through flowers, shrubs and trees.

The lawnmower rumbles as Daddy mows the lawn.
When he finishes, I lie down to rest and yawn!

Allah Gave Me Two Ears to Hear

The farm animals as they call to their young,
The cow moos to her calf who is having such fun.

N-n-neigh goes the horse, the chicken goes cluck,
The sheep go ba-a-a, and quack goes the duck.

Allah Gave Me Two Ears to Hear

The merry voices of my friends in the playground!
I scream with joy on the slide all the way down!

The rain as it gushes down during a storm!
I gather my toys and run to my home.

Allah Gave Me Two Ears to Hear

The beat of the daff in my rhythmic nasheeds
About loving Allah and doing good deeds.

The sweet sound of Daddy when he calls the adhan.
I make wudu and pray as soon as I can.

Allah Gave Me Two Ears to Hear

The deep purr of my striped furry cat.
I stroke him as he lies on my prayer mat.

The sound of cheery, joyous giggles.
As I tickle my brother, he squirms and wriggles!

Allah Gave Me Two Ears to Hear

The telephone shrills with a loud ring!
I run to the phone, 'I'll get it!' I sing.

Grandma's loving voice on the phone.
I wish she could be here from dusk' til dawn.

Allah Gave Me Two Ears to Hear

When my parents tell me they love me,
That always fills me with such joy and glee!

And the soothing sound of my Mummy's melody.
She puts me to sleep as I cuddle my teddy.

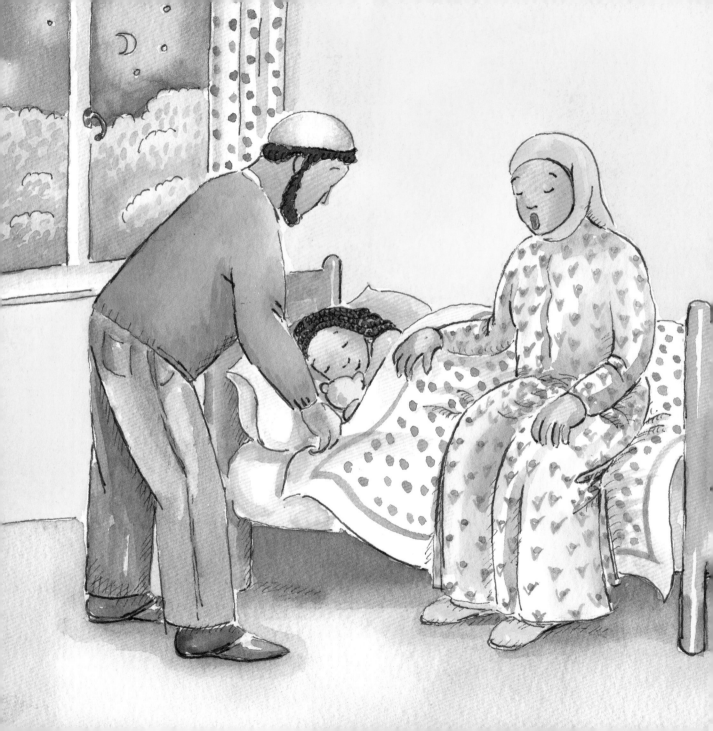

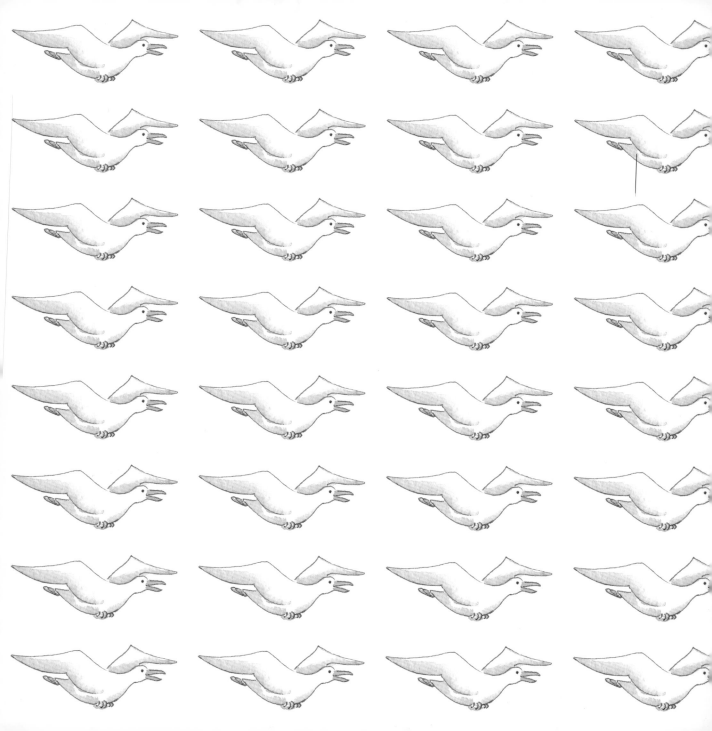